KATE GREENAWAY'S
BIRTHDAY
COLORING BOOK

WITH VERSES BY
MRS. SALE BARKER

PICTURES RENDERED FOR COLORING BY
NANCY PERKINS

DOVER PUBLICATIONS, INC., NEW YORK

PUBLISHER'S NOTE

The pictures in this book are copies of those the famous English artist Kate Greenaway (1846-1901) created for her miniature *Birthday Book* almost one hundred years ago. Her charming tiny pictures were an immediate and enormous success with the public, to such an extent that many parents adopted for their own children's wardrobe the quaint early nineteenth-century style of clothing she featured.

Ever since that time, the book has remained very popular. Hundreds of thousands of copies have been printed, and several generations of children have used it to record the birthdates of their friends, relatives and famous people they came to know and respect through study and reading.

By carefully enlarging the illustrations, our artist, Nancy Perkins, has added a new dimension to Miss Greenaway's book: now you can have the additional fun of coloring a picture almost every time you make a new entry in this book. [The box next to each date provides space in which you can record the name of up to four persons who were born on that day.] In this way, little by little your book will become more beautiful and meaningful. You will want to keep it for many years to remind you of all your good friends.

Kate Greenaway's Birthday Coloring Book, first published by Dover Publications, Inc., in 1974, contains enlarged and slightly modified copies of all of Kate Greenaway's illustrations for her *Birthday Book,* originally published circa 1880. This work also contains all the original verses by Mrs. Sale Barker.

DOVER *Pictorial Archive* SERIES

Kate Greenaway's Birthday Coloring Book belongs to the Dover Pictorial Archive Series. Up to ten illustrations from this book may be reproduced on any one project or in any single publication, free and without special permission. Wherever possible please include a credit line indicating the title of this book, author, and publisher. Please address the publisher for permission to make more extensive use of illustrations in this book than that authorized herein.

The republication of this book in whole is prohibited.

International Standard Book Number: 0-486-23050-3
Manufactured in the United States of America
Dover Publications, Inc.
180 Varick Street
New York, N.Y. 10014

BIRTHDAY
COLORING BOOK

JANUARY 1

What are the bells about? what do
 they say?
Ringing so sweetly for glad New
 Year's Day;
Telling us all that Time never will
 wait,
Bidding us use it well, ere it's too
 late.

JANUARY 2

A large brown muff, for cold, cold
 hands,
So dainty, too, trimmed up with
 bows;
Of all comforts the best, when you
 have to go out,
On a day when it freezes or blows.

JANUARY 3

There was an old woman who shook,
The wind her umbrella it took;
    She cried, "The wind's strong,
    I can't hold it long;"
And that's why she trembled and
 shook.

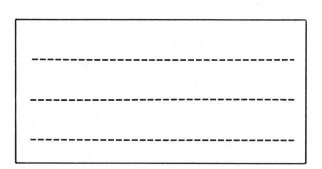

JANUARY 4

A great big muff and feathered
    hat,
    Poor little legs look bare;
A curious little figure this,
    Enough to make you stare.

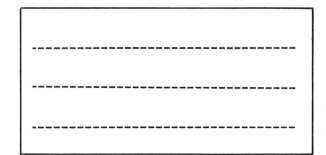

JANUARY 5

The joys of the tea-pot who will not
    sing?
The warmest and cosiest
    comforting thing!
Who does not enjoy a good cup of
    tea?
Without taste or reason I'm sure
    they must be.

JANUARY 6

So bright, so fresh, so delightfully
    nice,
To skim along on the hard smooth
    ice!
What fun to fly on your skates away,
Skating so gaily the whole of the
    day!

Jennifer

JANUARY 7

Old Mrs. Big-bonnet, little Miss
    Wee,
Out for an airing, as you may see;
Chatter and chatter, and pleasantly
    talk,
Enjoying together their nice
    winter's walk.

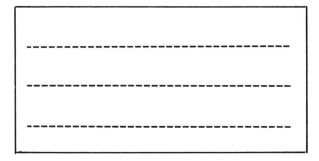

JANUARY 8

Who wouldn't go to a Fancy Ball?
High-heeled shoes to make us tall;
Ribbons, and laces, and powdered
    head,
And then to dance a minuet led.

JANUARY 9

I've seen many scarecrows, and
    Guys a few,
And I think this a frightful Guy —
    don't you?
Just look at her bonnet, and look at
    her back!
To dress herself well she hasn't
    the knack.

JANUARY 10

A Turk with a turban, I declare!
I think this will make you little
    ones stare.
Perhaps he's the Sultan, come
    over to see
If he in this Birthday Book will be.

JANUARY 11

Dear little Baby! he's wrapped up
    so warm,
And just beginning to run:
Out in the frosty day, roses to win,
Fresh air, and plenty of fun.

JANUARY 12

A jug and a basin — for what, do
  you think?
With water to wash little fingers
  from ink;
For some little children, alas! are
  so
Fond of touching such things, you
  know.

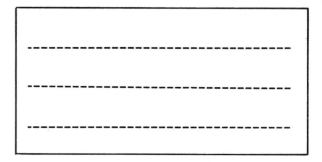

JANUARY 13

Roly-Poly with a snowball,
Throwing it at nothing at all;
Roly-Poly round about,
It seems to me he's very stout.

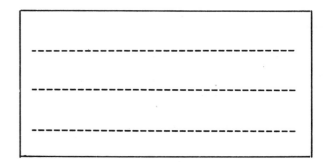

JANUARY 14

So wearied with her heavy load!
  So ragged, sad, and cold!
Dear children, always pity show
  To those who're poor and old.

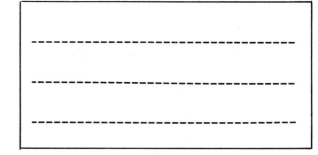

JANUARY 15

A clown, or a jester, I fancy this
  man,
But really I can't be sure, think as
  I can;
His hair stands on end, and his
  waist's very long,
And he looks just as if he were
  singing a song!

JANUARY 16

A cottage so rustic, and pretty, and
    warm;
    Would you like to live in it, pray?
Little children, I dare say, are
    living there now,
    And, though poor, are happy all
    day.

JANUARY 17

My dear little lady, now why turn
    your back?
    I am sure that your face is fair;
Yet we see but your dress, and the
    round of your cap,
    Not even a vestige of hair.

JANUARY 18

If you have cows, here's something
    to feed them,
    Something most juicy and sweet;
A fine mangold-wurzel is what cows
    delight in,
    To them 'tis a wonderful treat.

JANUARY 19

Small black-haired child, with a
    chubby round face,
    Two little round eyes, and round
    nose;
Little fat arms, and little white
    frock,
    And out peep the dear little toes!

JANUARY 20

There was an old woman whose hat
Was all peaked, and not at all flat;
   On her back was a hump,
   That stuck out in a lump, —
'Twas a trouble to her when she sat.

JANUARY 21

Of an empty chair, when it's ugly,
   too,
Why, what can we say, between me
   and you?
We only can fancy some lady fair
Is coming to sit in the empty chair.

JANUARY 22

A very grand lady, come out for a
   walk:
   What a feather, and large-
   brimmed hat!
So very important, yet only a child, —
   We all very well can see that.

JANUARY 23

At what a quick pace he is rushing
   along!
   Just look at his nose and his chin!
His hat, and his pig-tail, his
   curious legs,
   And his arms, too, so awkward
   and thin .

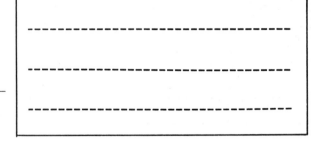

JANUARY 24

Pray, young lady, where are you
            going? —
      Out for a winter's walk;
To breathe fresh air, and come
            home fair,
      And then some tea and talk?

JANUARY 25

Useful and ornamental too,
      Handsome in colour and form
Cream-jugs may peaceful and
            pleasant be
      Though tea-pots sometimes have
            a storm.

JANUARY 26

Sitting by the fireside, thinking of
            the past,
Of the time, long faded now, far too
            bright to last;
Waiting patiently and still, for the
            end to come,
Looking — with what wistful eyes! —
            for the last long home.

JANUARY 27

This woman is going to market,
      With a basket full of eggs:
She has many a weary mile to walk,
      I pity her tired legs.

7

JANUARY 28

Goosey, goosey, gander!
    With a night-cap on his head;
He turns himself, and twists
    himself,
    And then he goes to bed.

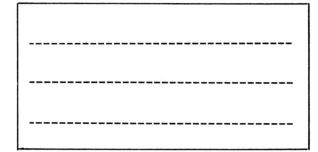

JANUARY 29

Footstool, or hassock, whichever
    you call it,
    Is useful enough in its way;
But it helps little people sometimes
    to a tumble,
    And big people, too, I may say.

JANUARY 30

What is he doing, this little Jack
    Horner;
    There on his three-legged stool?
Is he doing his lessons, or eating
    his dinner
    Or merely just playing the fool?

JANUARY 31

Baby is looking for father,
    He's been such a long time away;
Father is coming to baby,
    Has thought of her all through the
    day.

FEBRUARY 1

Is this Queen Elizabeth, may I ask,
    With her ruff, and her cushioned
    head?
No, for this lady still proudly walks,
    And Queen Elizabeth's dead..

FEBRUARY 2

Cabbages red, and cabbages green,
This is a fine one as ever was seen:
Cabbages grow in the garden near,
Cabbages grow the whole of the
    year.

FEBRUARY 3

This is Master Baby, paying a
    morning call,
Sitting so good upon his chair, but
    speaking not at all;
Listening to every word, the funny
    little man!
Wondering at the news he hears,
    thinking all he can.

FEBRUARY 4

Hush-a-bye, Dolly! go to your rest;
    Mother wants to be busy, you
    know.
Dolly, be quiet, I won't have you cry;
    To sleep, child, you really must
    go.

FEBRUARY 5

A nice new broom, to sweep away,
   And keep the floor so clean;
The crumbs and dust all disappear,
   There's not one to be seen.

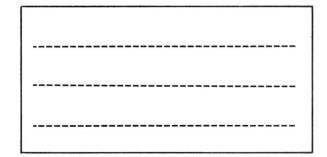

FEBRUARY 6

The wind, determined to have
   some fun,
Blew an old woman to make her run;
The old woman trotted along with
   a will,
But stopped at last, when she got
   to a hill.

FEBRUARY 7

A kite, one day, flew up in the sky,
   To try and reach the sun;
He failed, and he fell with a broken
   string,
And sighed, "It can't be done!"

FEBRUARY 8

There was an old person too fat,
Who wore a remarkable hat;
   He said, "Let the world talk,
   I'll take a good walk,
And try to get rid of this fat."

FEBRUARY 9

A shuttlecock was sent so high,
He very nearly reached the sky;
When he came down he was so vain,
They never sent him up again.

FEBRUARY 10

Little maid, little maid, whither
away,
Running so fast on this early-spring
day?
Perhaps it's Mamma you are going
to meet,
And Love lends his wings to your
little feet.

FEBRUARY 11

Turnips and carrots are all very
fine,
If on boiled mutton you're going
to dine;
But, as that is a dish that I really
can't bear,
I'll willingly give up to you all my
share.

FEBRUARY 12

A pot of spring flowers before me
stands,
Primroses fresh and fair;
Telling of days that are coming
soon,
When their sweetness fills the air.

FEBRUARY 13

Carrying home the washing,
　Snowy-white and clean;
Merry maidens bring it home,
　As can well be seen.

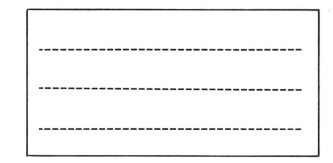

FEBRUARY 14

Pray, little lady, why do you come
　　out,
　When it's raining in this way?
Perhaps an important letter to
　　post? —
　I remember, it's Valentine's Day!

FEBRUARY 15

Johnnie has got a new peg-top,
　That spins with wonderful grace;
The boy is surprised and delighted,
　Just look in his eager face.

FEBRUARY 16

Polly, the milkmaid, comes over
　　the plain,
　Fills up her milk-pail, and then
　　back again;
Milk for our breakfast, milk for
　　our tea,
　Thank the good moo-cows for you
　　and for me.

12

FEBRUARY 17

The old pump stands in the
  meadow,
Where all the cows are fed, O!
To give them a drink is but fair,
  I think,
So the old pump stands in the
  meadow.

FEBRUARY 18

Little Laura Lazy lies against
  the wall;
If she spends her time so, she'll do
  no work at all,
Softly we will touch her, give a
  little shake,
Then, perhaps, this idle maid may
  think it time to wake.

FEBRUARY 19

Little Tom Thumbkin blows bubbles
  so light,
Up they go — higher yet — colours
  so bright;
Little Tom Thumbkin looks quite
  forlorn —
His bubbles die as soon as they're
  born.

FEBRUARY 20

An empty chair! an empty chair!
Come and sit down on it, any who
  dare;
It looks so firm, but give it a
  shake,
And into pieces it soon will break.

13

FEBRUARY 21

"Little friend, little friend, why
    stare you so?"
"I'm looking, I'm looking, to see
    the wind blow."
"Little friend, little friend, have
    you a mind
To become a small pig? They alone
    see the wind."

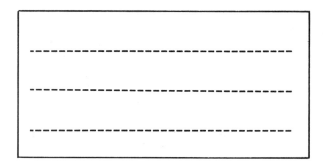

FEBRUARY 22

A good-sized bonnet, a very small
    dog,
    As you can plainly see;
The bonnet would do for a kennel
    too,
    It really seems to me.

FEBRUARY 23

"Baker, what have you got in your
    basket?
    Something good, I trust,"
"Cakes and buns, jam tarts and
    biscuits,
    Pastry with nice thin crust."

FEBRUARY 24

A Japanese tea-pot! let's have
    some tea,
A cup of the most delicious bohea!
Then plenty of sugar, and plenty
    of cream,
And with smiles of contentment our
    faces will beam.

FEBRUARY 25

"Dolly, Dolly, tell me, dear,
    Do you like your ride?
The go-cart's small, but so are you,
    There's room for more beside."

FEBRUARY 26

Do, pray, look at this lazy loon,
Smoking his pipe before it's noon!
Leaning his back against a rail,
While the little black dog is wagging
    his tail.

FEBRUARY 27

Selina Amelia called out to her cat,—
"Oh, Pussy, dear Pussy, I wish you'd
    grow fat;
Here's a saucer of milk, mixed with
    oil from the cod,
I hope you won't think that the
    mixture is odd."

FEBRUARY 28

Shall I sing to my baby about the
    bright flowers?
    Shall I sing about the glad sun?
Shall I sing to my baby of long
    summer hours?
    Shall I sing to my sweet little one?

------- Marcia -------

FEBRUARY 29

A green, green tree, that stands by
itself,
A tree without very much shade;
For its branches are cropped quite
small at top,
Until to a point it is made.

MARCH 1

Not much to be seen but a feather!
Can it be on account of the weather?
We'll suppose a fine face,
And a great deal of grace,
So hidden because of the weather.

MARCH 2

Upright as a dart, but without much
grace,
And her grandmother's bonnet quite
hides her face.
I can't say much for her — now,
can you?
And I shouldn't care to say, How
do you do?

MARCH 3

Now, this I call a feat of skill,
Though I should think it made him
ill,
To catch a ball, and stand like that,
Above all, when one's rather fat.

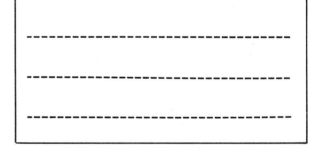

Daddy

MARCH 4

Miss Roundabout's dressed to go to
    a ball,
You'd think her so stout that she
    can't dance at all;
But she is so light, she's just like
    a balloon,
And thinks that each dance is over
    too soon.

MARCH 5

Little Kitty, how I love you!
I like to squeeze you to my cheek;
Always purring, never scratching,
Always gentle, always meek.

MARCH 6

I was walking in the country,
    It was a little sad;
This was the only creature near,
    The only friend I had.

MARCH 7

Vain young person, who may
    you be,
Turning your head to look at me?
I will give you a penny, or give
    you a bun;
But compliments from me, you
    will have none.

MARCH 8

What is she looking at, up in the
  sky,
Is it the moon or the sun?
She will be dazzled, or moonstruck,
  perhaps.
And then, what is to be done?

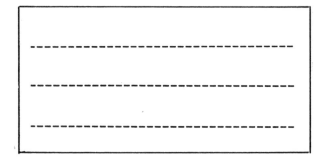

MARCH 9

Here is a round ball, give it to me,
And I will toss it up high;
Forty times as high as the house,
Then will it reach the sky?

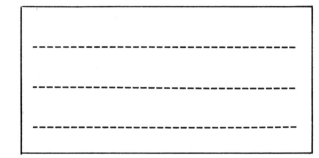

MARCH 10

Alack! alas! and well-a-day!
Here's never a child come out to
  play;
I'll tell Belinda, Clarissa, and Jane,
I never will promise to meet them
  again.

MARCH 11

In this little wee house an old
  woman dwells,
She makes gingerbread figures, and
  lollipops sells;
The children all cheer her wherever
  she goes,
But she has a great trouble —
  which is a red nose.

MARCH 12

"Polly, what are you looking at?
  What do you see out there?"
"I see a ship sailing far, far off;
  And where is it going?" — Ah,
    where?

MARCH 13

A little Marionnette man,
  Throwing up a ball;
I really cannot understand
  How he can catch at all.

MARCH 14

Dear little maid! — Is she sleeping,
  Or crying her woes to the ground?
Grief, and rest, and a little joy, —
  It is thus the world goes round.

MARCH 15

Baby, baby, in the bowl,
  Have you caught an eel?
Only cotton for a line,
  To fish for Mother's reel.

19

MARCH 16

Little Miss Sarsenet looks very
glum;
Do you think that she's cross and
sulky? — Hum!
It may be so, or it may not be;
Miss Sarsenet's slightly ruffled,
I see.

MARCH 17

Sweet are the hedges close to the
stile
Laden with blossoms of May;
Sweet sings the river that murmurs
below
The whole of the happy spring
day.

MARCH 18

Poor little wandering gipsy child,
In rags, with feet all bare!
Come, bring some meat, and bread,
and cake,
And let her have a share.

MARCH 19

This is the woman who is so fat,
There is no door she can get in at;
She has a child, so very small,
That it can scarce be seen at all.

MARCH 20

Strike away! strike away!
Make the hoop run:
The faster it rolls.
The greater the fun.

MARCH 21

Two loving little sisters, going for
a walk,
Chatter, chatter gaily, pleasantly
they talk;
What do they talk of? Dolls,
politics, and bees;
Both have the same views — that
one plainly sees.

MARCH 22

Benevolent and happy man,
Who takes his walks abroad;
He gives away his pence and pounds
And all he can afford.

MARCH 23

Who is coming to Margery?
Who is coming, I say?
Some dearly loved one, who brings
a plum bun, —
That's who is coming, I say.

MARCH 24

The wind blew hard, the wind blew
strong,
And blew Lucinda fast along;
At last it blew her up in the air,
Now, has she come down, or is she
still there?

MARCH 25

Ah! sweet primrose, you are come,
To tell us of the Spring;
The hedge-rows bloom, the woods
are green,
And now the birdies sing.

MARCH 26

Little Patty is delighted,
What, do you think, about?
All the flowers are shooting up
And all the buds are out.

MARCH 27

Poor Miss Baby, in the wind,
Finds herself unsteady,
And she has to trot alone,
Until Nurse is ready.

MARCH 28

Lily of the Valley, very fair to see,
Sweet and dear to all I've loved,
          ever dear to me.
Flower, pure and fragrant, when you
          begin your reign
Visions of a glad lost time will
          ever come again.

MARCH 29

Small Billy is a coachman
          But where — oh! where's his
          team?
I think they're gone to Fairyland,
          Or vanished in a dream.

MARCH 30

The sails go round with a heavy
          swing
          As the wild wind plays on the hill;
And the corn is crushed, and the
          flour ground
          Right merrily at the mill.

MARCH 31

What does the child see? — is it
          the moon?
Or does she look at an air balloon?
Up yet higher, ever so far,
Out there peeps the evening star.

APRIL 1

Look at this boy as you pass by;
Look, how he's laughing! I'll tell
you why:
He made an old woman an April
fool:
With vulgar boys that is the rule.

APRIL 2

A pot of flowers, if you are able,
Always have upon the table;
And a bird who'll sweetly sing:
These things tell you of the spring.

APRIL 3

Baby dear, with eyes so bright,
Staring up with all your might!
What is the sight, or what the sound,
That makes your eyes so big
and round?

APRIL 4

I am walking out so early,
To see my great-aunt Jane;
I'll walk a mile, and talk a while,
And then come home again.

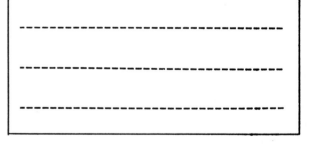

APRIL 5

Daffodils grow in the meadows,
  Scenting the April air:
Daffodils out in the garden, —
  I'm glad I have them there.

APRIL 6

Running along with his flag in
    his hand,
  To frighten the cows away;
We see but his back, and the crown
    of his hat,
  His face, p'rhaps, some other day.

APRIL 7

A Normandy peasant, come out
    for a walk:
Could you understand if you heard
    her talk?
"Bon jour, joli enfant," she
    would say,
Which means, "Pretty child, I wish
    you good-day."

APRIL 8

Rushes by the river-side,
  Growing proud and tall;
The wind comes by, and makes
    them bow,
  Then they look quite small.

APRIL 9

Baby, with the tea-cup,
What have you got in it?
If it is tea, give it to me;
Come, share it, miss, this
minute.

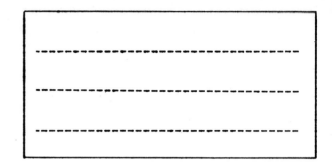

APRIL 10

Up the rope, up the rope,
Ever so high!
Will you come down again?
"Yes, by-and-by."

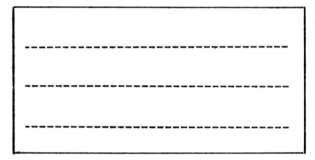

APRIL 11

Birdie, dear birdie, oh, whence
do you come?
Now say, do you bring any news?
Has mother come back from
London town,
And has she not brought me
new shoes?

Suzana

APRIL 12

What's in the basket, the basket?
What is there, great or small?
Perhaps plum buns and gingerbread,
Perhaps there's none at all.

APRIL 13

Cowslips, cowslips, fresh and sweet,
    And very, very dear!
I look at you, and then go back —
    Oh, many a long, long year!

APRIL 14

Mermaid, or child in a sea-shell?
Pray, little mermaid, is that where
    you dwell?
Blown by the wind, riding over
    the sea,
I'd rather it you, little mermaid,
    than me.

APRIL 15

Little hands behind you!
    And why do you hide them, then?
Have you a ball, or nothing at all
    But fat little fingers ten?

APRIL 16

Would you like to know why I walk
    so fast?
    A sight I'm going to see;
It may be a ship, or it may be a
    shark. —
    It may, or it may not be.

APRIL 17

Upon the grass, beneath the bright
    spring sunshine,
    There sat a gentle, pensive
      little maid;
The soft spring air just breathed a
    perfume near her,
    "I bring the kisses of the
      flowers," it said.

APRIL 18

Who went in the fields to-day,
To gather marigolds, I say?
Was it Belinda Abiathar Ann?
Tell me, I pray you, if you can.

APRIL 19

Dear me! this is very odd,
    Upon the stairs to sit;
I think she's got her night-gown on,
    And doesn't care a bit.

APRIL 20

I want to see the world, you know;
    I'm going to be a sailor:
This is my sailor suit, you see,
    Just come home from the tailor.

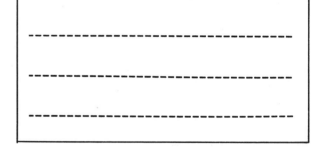

APRIL 21

Come and look at this round plate,
Hanging alone in pomp and state.
Do you like it empty, or covered
    with cake?
I hope it's not always like this, for
    your sake.

APRIL 22

"Little girl, where do you come
    from?
    Little girl, where do you go?"
"I come from the school in
    the hollow,
    Where they teach us to read and
    to sew."

PaPa

APRIL 23

Yes, I am fond of them;
Now, are not you? —
Fond of potatoes,
When they are new?

APRIL 24

There was an old woman whose
    mind
Was fixed on a race with the wind;
    Her friends said, "You'll find
    You'll be soon left behind;"
But she smiled, and set off with
    the wind.

APRIL 25

Have you got a cabbage there,
Little funny maiden fair?
"Yes, I have, I'm going to boil it,
Though the cook says I shall
spoil it."

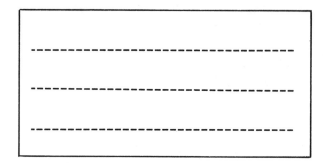

APRIL 26

See, O children! now I bring
Glad sweet flowers of the spring:
May your paths with flowers
be spread
May you on them lightly tread!

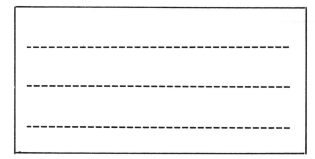

APRIL 27

Just an entrance, nothing more;
Whither, whither does it go? —
Where glad hearts are gay and light,
Or where they ache in silent
woe?

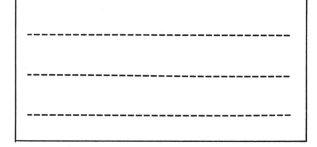

APRIL 28

Ivy, stealthily you creep,
Killing where you cling.
Strange! so graceful, fair a plant,
Should be a cruel thing.

APRIL 29

Blowing airy bubbles light,
Watching changing colours bright:
Tommy, happy as a king,
Joyful at so small a thing.

APRIL 30

Yes, they did squabble, *scratched*
    in their spite;
Now they are friends again —
    friends again quite,
Look, how they lovingly each give a
    kiss;
Now we are sure that there's not
    much amiss.

MAY 1

A strange-looking creature as ever
    was seen,
Dancing and grinning round
    Jack-in-the-green;
This is an old fashion, that comes
    in with May,
And sad for the sweeps if the First's
    a wet day.

MAY 2

"Here's a nest," said a bird.
    "With my eggs in it, three;
All spotted and handsome,
    As eggs can well be."

MAY 3

Tulips in the garden grow,
    Don't they make it gay?
I'm very fond of tulips,
    I'll pick one if I may.

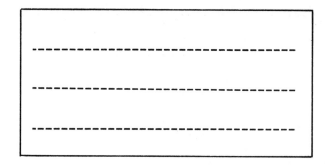

MAY 4

Little airy, fairy sprite,
    Flying in the air;
Dropping blossoms to the earth,
    Scattering flowerets fair.

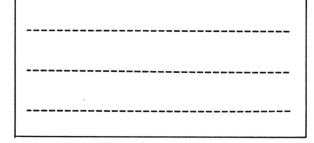

MAY 5

Is she sad, little maid,
    Or is she but sleeping?
I'd rather she dozed,
    Than made eyes red by weeping.

MAY 6

When I was out a-walking,
    I met an old, old man;
What he said, and what I said,
    Now, guess it if you can.

MAY 7

Come, jump off the tub — just let
    me see
If you can do it; now — one,
    two, three!
Yes, you have done it; let's
    merrily run
Out to the fields, and we'll have
    fine fun.

MAY 8

This girl is dressed all
    spick-and-span,
And neatly as can be;
Her sash well tied, her mittens
    straight,
She's going out to tea.

MAY 9

Wild roses grow in hedges,
    In the merry summer-time,
I've talked of them, and sung of them,
    And put them into rhyme.

MAY 10

Watching how the daisies grow,
    In the early morning;
At night their yellow eyes are closed,
    But open in the dawning

MAY 11

"Paddy, oh Paddy, now where
　　do you go,
Stepping an Irish jig, dancing
　　just so?"
"Oh, shure I'm off, then, to Dublin
　　town,
To buy wife and children aich a
　　new gown."

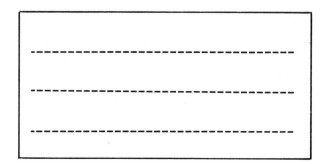

MAY 12

Blossoms pink, and blossoms white,
　　Flowering in May;
Sweet and bright, they bloom so fair,
　　And all the world is gay.

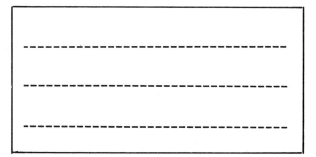

MAY 13

Such a big bonnet, a basket as big!
Is she going to market to buy a
　　small pig?
When she comes back, it will be a
　　fine joke,
A pig in a basket, a child in a poke.

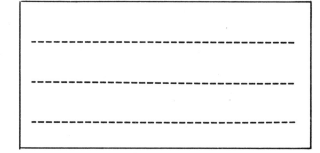

MAY 14

Up, up flies the shuttlecock, up with
　　a jump,
Down on the battledore now, with
　　a thump.
Fly away, shuttlecock, higher yet
　　fly,
Up to the clouds that pass over
　　the sky.

MAY 15

A spirit floating through the night,
Where the stars now shed their
light.
Tell us, tell us what you are?
The Spirit of the Evening Star.

MAY 16

Tulips in a pot, you see;
Phillis brought them in to me;
I thought Phillis very kind,
To pick her one I'd half a mind.

MAY 17

Little Peggie has a dicky, and it
is very tame;
She loves her bird — oh, dearly!
and it loves her just the same;
She gives it lots of breadcrumbs,
a lump of sugar, too:
I wish I had a bird like that, I'm
sure, and so do you.

MAY 18

Now, make haste, and go to school,
Don't loiter here all day:
A girl should walk quite fast to
school,
And hurry on her way.

MAY 19

Carry the baby over the fields,
Carry her up the high hill;
Carry her here, and carry her there,
For baby will never be still.

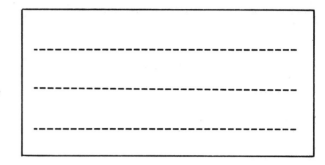

MAY 20

There was an old person
who feared
The sun setting light to his beard;
So he said, "I will see, and sit
under a tree
Till the sun is too low to
be feared."

MAY 21

Do you want to hear the news?
I am dancing without shoes;
I can dance, and I can run,
I am up to any fun.

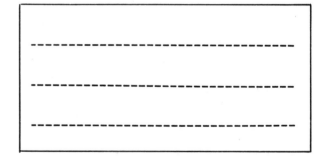

MAY 22

A sweet, sweet sprig of
lily-of-the-valley
Who shall have it? Little merry
Sally;
She shall keep it; and wear it
all day:
Lilies are found in the garden
in May.

MAY 23

This is Wilhelmina's back, who
    looks so neat and nice,
Of bread-and-butter she will take,
    at tea, but one small slice;
And when she is invited to take
    a little more,
She always answers softly, "I had
    too much before."

MAY 24

Out comes a fledgling, out of
    his shell;
He's out in the world, but he won't
    see it well;
For off on his journey he's come
    but one mile,
And thinks he'll go back again, to
    rest awhile.

MAY 25

I have a young canary,
    And he loves most to dine
On fresh green dandelion leaves,
    When they are young and fine.

MAY 26

Round you go, skipping-rope,
    over I fly;
Which is the happiest, think,
    you or I?
I am the happiest, 'tis by my will
That I skip over you, or I stand still.

MAY 27

Little Bobby Balancer walks
    upon a rail,
If he slips and has a fall — ah!
    then his walks will fail;
If he keeps his balance, and touches
    not the ground,
Then Bobby'll reach his home again,
    lucky, safe, and sound!

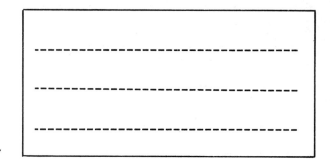

MAY 28

This is Joan, she is all alone,
The others have gone to the fair;
She is rather sad, for it seems
    too bad
That poor Joan should not also
    be there.

MAY 29

This is little baby's back,
    Isn't it full of grace?
But you'd know how sweet she is,
    If you saw her face.

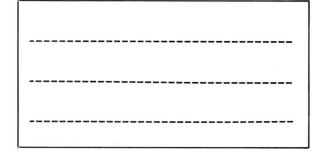

MAY 30

What is he doing, that fat boy,
    With a bonnet on his head?
He's a lazy loon, this afternoon;
    I should send him off to bed.

MAY 31

Little wild flower, that grows
in the field,
Ringing your merry bell!
What do you say in that tiny
chime? —
Pray, little flower, tell.

JUNE 1

Windmills, like weathercocks, turn
with the wind,
And change, as indeed they may;
Some little folks are exactly
the same,
Perhaps this is their birthday!

JUNE 2

This weak little girl sheds a tear,
She quakes and she trembles
with fear;
But it's only a fish, though not
in a dish,
So she need not display such
great fear.

JUNE 3

Warm little hearts, and wise
little heads,
Gentle, and loving, and kind;
This is the way to be happy, small
friends,
And that you will very soon find.

JUNE 4

A rose in June, a rose in June,
    That scents the summer air!
In blooming pink, I really think,
    Of flowers you are most fair.

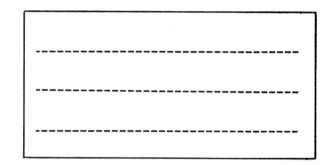

JUNE 5

Baby, baby, you look like a mouse,
Holding a bonnet as big as a house.
Now, is it Granny's you've
        borrowed just now?
Do you think you may keep it? —
        will Granny allow?

JUNE 6

Blossoms, blossoms on the trees
Swinging in the summer breeze,
Lending sweetness to the air,
To be shed on children fair.

JUNE 7

This is Melinda, who sits all
        day long,
Thoughtful and pensive, composing
        a song.
None wish to hear it, so people say
It is not much use her composing
        this lay.

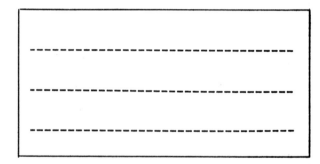

JUNE 8

A little girl jumped for joy,
  Upon the eighth of June;
She cried, "My birthday's come
    at last,
  But it will go too soon."

JUNE 9

Inside the window, a lady;
  Outside, a rose-tree grows;
Kind is the beautiful lady,
  Sweet is the creeping rose.

JUNE 10

I'm rather idle, as you see,
  I sit upon the ground;
And all the world seems made
    for me
  As it turns round and round.

JUNE 11

Yes, it is sad indeed, — sad, I
    must say it;
That there's no croquet now, no
    one will play it.
Here stands Selina, with mallet
    and ball;
But no one will come and play,
    no one at all.

JUNE 12

Ride away, ride on the branch
of a tree;
How your horse canters, with
action so free!
Don't ride too far, remember
we're here:
Come back and tell us your travels,
my dear.

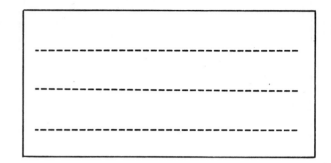

JUNE 13

Gorgeous sunflower, yellow and
bright,
Turning your face to the sun;
Glorying, basking in his glad light,
Until his day's work is done.

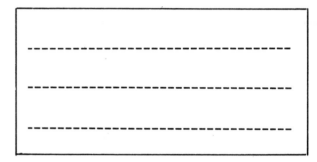

JUNE 14

A little girl, a little girl,
Once went to pick some flowers;
They said, "Oh, pray go home again,
We're sure to have some
showers."

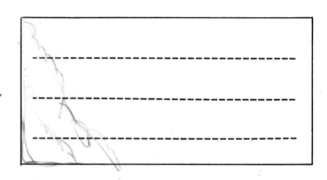

JUNE 15

A carnation in our garden grows;
How pleased we are to know it!
Our gardener said we should
have one,
He said, "I'm going to sow it."

JUNE 16

A pretty tree, a shady tree,
  Just casts its shadow round;
And we can go and sit beneath,
  If we don't mind the ground.

JUNE 17

Janet plays at ball all day,
  Through the hot, hot weather;
Her ball is small, but very hard,
  Because it's made of leather.

JUNE 18

Tiger-lily, tall and straight,
  How handsomely you grow!
Your spotted leaves, and
    yellow tongues —
  But stop! — you're vain, I know.

JUNE 19

Margery has a new skipping rope,
  Margery skips all the day;
Bobby and Bill hate the skipping,
  For Margery with them
    won't play.

JUNE 20

Little girl leaning against the stile,
Are you resting yourself awhile?
Do you think — how sweet is the
summer day,
When all the world seems
made for play?

JUNE 21

Little flower of the field,
To me you tell a tale,
Of blooms upon the hill-side,
Of blossoms in the vale.

JUNE 22

This girl is walking to London town,
Her luncheon in her basket;
She's walking, walking up and down,
Her way — she'll have to ask it.

JUNE 23

Dear moon-daisies, I love you;
Old friends, that I know so well;
Glad scenes come back when I
see you,
And sad thoughts that I dare
not tell.

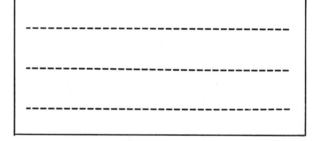

MaMa

JUNE 24

Poppy, poppy, flaunting red,
    In the meadow green;
You are so bold, you stare about,
    And you are always seen.

JUNE 25

Against a post leant Tabitha,
    Her fan within her hand;
She looked about, did Tabitha,
    And she surveyed the land.

JUNE 26

These are the two Miss Minevers,
    So good, so very good!
They each do what the other likes,
    As sisters always should.

JUNE 27

I am a mountain daffodil,
    My colour it is yellow;
I think the whole world must agree
    I am a handsome fellow.

JUNE 28

This is a house, it's very straight,
 And also rather tall;
And lovers of the picturesque
 Don't like this house at all.

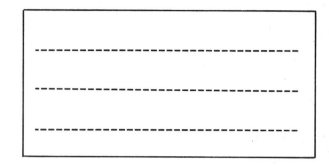

JUNE 29

This flower grows within my garden,
 Perhaps you have the same;
If that's the case, of course you
 know it,
 Pray therefore, tell its name.

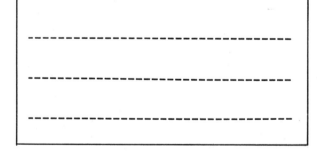

JUNE 30

There was a young person whose
 passion
Was always to dress in the fashion;
 That she did not succeed,
 To tell there's no need,
For you see that she's *not* in
 the fashion.

JULY 1

There she goes with her pitchfork,
 To turn about the hay,
To toss it up, and spread it out,
 On this hot summer day.

JULY 2

This is a beautiful Iris,
  Soft purple is its hue;
I think it a grand-looking flower,
  Now tell me, do not you?

JULY 3

Michael

The sweetest, freshest, pinkest
    rose!
  The rose-tree in our garden
    grows,
It is sweet to sight and smell;
  Indeed, we love that rose-tree
    well.

JULY 4

I lie beside the running stream,
And watch the clouds, and rest,
    and dream:
A jug with water by me stands,
Which I have filled with my
    own hands.

JULY 5

Sitting on the wall!
It is not safe at all.
Come, come, get down, I say;
You can't sit there all day.

JULY 6

How I love the field flowers,
    Blooming bright and gay!
How I love the green, green fields,
    To wander there all day!

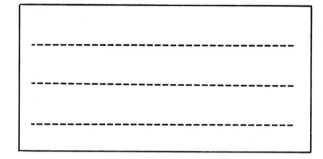

JULY 7

Most certainly I hardly know
    If she has doll or baby;
Perhaps you know, you are so wise.
    And think me but a gaby.

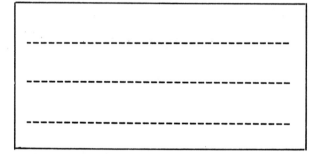

JULY 8

That girl has got a large round hat,
    Perhaps a round red face;
We cannot judge how this may be,
    But only of her grace.

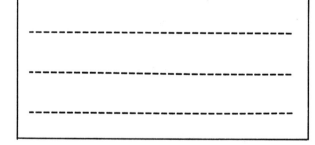

JULY 9

Currants black, and currants red,
    Let's have some in a pie,
With sugar and delicious cream —
    We'll have some by-and-by.

JULY 10

Letty and Etty walked hand in hand,
Pleasantly, quietly through the
broad land;
Letty and Etty said, "Are we
not good?
We walk and we talk just as little
girls should."

JULY 11

Lily, Lily, white and tall,
You are wondrous fair;
I bid you welcome to this book,
I'm glad you're standing there.

JULY 12

Little Phillipina stands to watch
the sun,
Thinks she'll stand and watch it till
its work is done;
Little Phillipina, you must watch
all day,
For the sun will shine till night,
and then he'll go away.

JULY 13

I look at this, and here is seen
A little sprig of creeping bean;
I like to eat them, I like them
growing,
I like them in this picture showing.

JULY 14

Do you like gooseberries? I
can't say I do;
Perhaps you like currants, and
raspberries too.
I wish you could come to our
country home;
How much in the garden you would
like to roam!

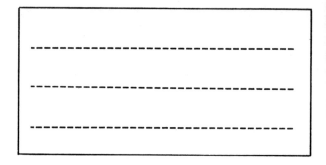

JULY 15

To market they go, on St.
Swithin's day,
They've something to sell, and
something to pay;
They've one big umbrella to keep
off the rain,
Which comes, on that Saint's day,
again and again.

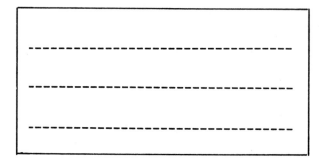

JULY 16

It's very sad to stand alone,
Upon a summer's day,
And long to see some chubby child,
To have a game at play.

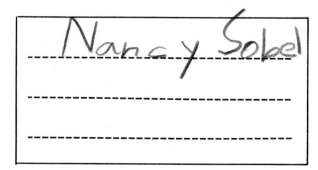

Nancy Sobel

JULY 17

A bramble once looked over a rail,
"We shall have some rain,"
she said;
"Well, it's time that the grass
should have a drink,
And it's time that the dust
was laid."

JULY 18

White and blue convolvulus!
　　At four it goes to bed,
With bell closed tight with all
　　　　its might,
　　Perhaps you've heard it said?

JULY 19

This funny old woman takes care
　　　　of her dog,
　　Her sun-shade protects her and it;
"It's the dog-days, you know, and
　　　　think, if poor Flo
　　Went mad," said she, "and
　　　　then bit!"

JULY 20

The shuttlecock up in the air
　　　　has flown,
Oh, where, and oh, where is it gone?
Alack and alack! will it never come
　　　　back?
The battledore's left all forlorn.

JULY 21

This is Johnny, who says, "I've
　　　　heard the hen cackle
　　　I'm sure that some eggs she
　　　　has laid;
I'll go to the hen-house, and fill
　　　　my basket —
　　　That is, if I don't feel afraid."

JULY 22

When we have the warm, warm
      sunshine,
   That is when the flowers grow;
In the garden, by the footpath,
   Stand the flowers in a row.

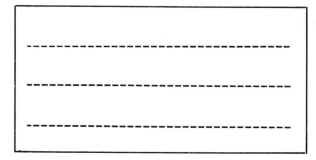

JULY 23

Up the post the rose-tree twines,
   With its blossoms sweet and fair;
To its neighbour lends a grace —
   To the post, so plain and bare.

JULY 24

Hurrah, hurrah, for harvest-time!
   Hurrah for the grain our land
      yields!
Hurrah, hurrah, for the
      harvest-home,
   For the yellow sheaves in
      the fields!

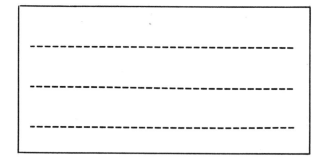

JULY 25

As I went out to take the air,
   I met two maidens small;
I greeted them politely,
   But they answered not at all.

JULY 26

A maiden went a-gleaning,
    Upon a summer's day;
She gleaned and gleaned a goodly
        sheaf
    Then went upon her way.

JULY 27

Tilly Toddles knocked her head
    A very hard, hard blow;
She loudly cried, and sadly sighed
    "Oh dear! it hurts me so!"

JULY 28

When I have no flowers, I love the
        leaves so green;
And the dainty leaf of a creeping
        plant is prettiest to be seen;
And if I can have flowers, with them
        I leaves entwine.
So round the clustering blossoms lie
        the leaves of the creeping vine.

JULY 29

This girl has got the baby, I hope
        she will take care;
I think she might forget it — forget
        that it is there.
She wears so large a bonnet, that
        she really cannot see;
And she might drop the baby, and
        then how sad 'twould be!

JULY 30

"My greatest delight," said
  Timothy White,
"Is to swing by my arms all day;
To me people call, 'Pray come down,
  you will fall;'
But I laugh, and continue my play."

JULY 31

Flowers yellow, leaves all green,
Here's a puffy ball between;
The children blow those balls away,
"They're clocks, and tell the time,"
  they say.

AUGUST 1

Here's a girl, she has a basket,
What is in it — do you ask it?
I heard a miow! it is a cat!
Now, children, what do you think
  of that?

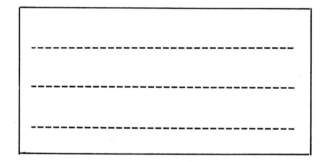

Rebecca K
Cornia

AUGUST 2

A small, small branch of a very
  large tree:
Pray, little folks, say what it may be?
It is shady and grand, and grows
  in our land,
And is reckoned a very fine tree.

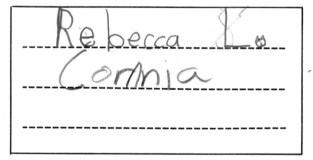

_____ Mommy _____

_____

_____

AUGUST 3

Tommy Thumbkin rides a barrel,—
  Where does his journey lead?
To No-where Town, which is miles
    away,
  He rides on his stalwart steed.

AUGUST 4

A pot of flowers — oh, how sweet,
Flowers always are a treat;
In a garden or a pot,
We all love flowers — do we not?

AUGUST 5

This tree grows in a garden,
  Where merry children run;
They like this funny little tree,
  It shelters them from sun.

AUGUST 6

This lady has come to pay a call,
  To have a little chat;
She talks of the weather, she talks
    of the news,
  She talks of this and of that.

AUGUST 7

Poor croquet balls! quite idle,
They've got no work to do;
Just like the frozen-out gardeners,
That in winter trouble you.

AUGUST 8

How doth the greedy little bee
Take honey to his hive;
And sting, and buzz, and much annoy,
And to be foremost strive.

AUGUST 9

What does little Johnny see? —
A waggon with horses four;
Each horse has a bell, and it
jingles well,
But Johnny wishes for more.

AUGUST 10

Plums, plums, purple plums!
Do you like them in a tart?
I like to pick them from the tree,
And eat them, for my part.

_____ Me _____

_____

_____

AUGUST 11

Flowers now are getting scarce,
　　I regret to say;
How very, very sad 'twill be.
　　When all are gone away!

_____

_____

_____

AUGUST 12

Upon a stile, beside a moor,
This boy sits quiet as a mouse;
He hears the sportsmen
　　shooting near,
They're killing all the little grouse.

_____

_____

_____

AUGUST 13

What is this boy staring at?
　　I dare say you wonder too;
Try as I may, I cannot say,
　　But it must be something new.

_____

_____

_____

AUGUST 14

A player at croquet at last,
So it's not quite a thing of the past;
This girl is quite ready, with mallet
　　in hand,
So I hope she won't have alone
　　long to stand.

AUGUST 15

This damsel seems extremely
proud,
Her nose so high in air;
I really don't think much of her,
Such pride I cannot bear.

AUGUST 16

What have you there, you dear
little girl?
What have you there, now tell?
Are they good, good things, you will
have for tea;
Or things that you want to sell?

AUGUST 17

Out in the garden Miss Peachblossom
ran,
A hat on her head, in her hand a
great fan;
"I smell the sweet flowers — a bird
past me flies;
Good-bye, pretty garden!" and
back she then hies.

AUGUST 18

Darling baby, as you look
Straight at me out of this book;
How I wish that I could take you,
And a real live baby make you.

_____ Christopher _____

AUGUST 19

A very small man, with cocked
hat so gay,
Remarkably active, he runs
fast away;
A neat little figure, compact, and
so brave,
As in triumph he lifts up his banner
to wave.

AUGUST 20

An Italian peasant, by a well;
Who she is I cannot tell;
She wears a very curious cap,
Awkward, if she took a nap.

AUGUST 21

A storm in a tea-pot, I declare!
Do tell me what's the matter!
This little person's quite put out,
That's why there's such a clatter.

AUGUST 22

A train goes by, and Tommy runs,
And holds a flag quite high;
It is such fun, small Tommy thinks,
To see a train go by.

AUGUST 23

This girl is waiting for somebody,
  For whom is she waiting, I say?
I think it's for the pedlar,
  Who often comes this way.

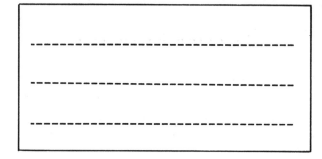

AUGUST 24

Peter is running, oh, running!
  And why does he run so fast?
He teased an old hen, who flew
    at him then,
  And he thinks she will catch him
    at last.

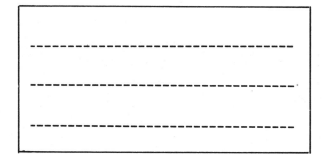

AUGUST 25

Eliza Jane she goes to market,
  Upon a market day:
You'd like to know why it is so?
  Well, really, I can't say.

AUGUST 26

An old person once said, "I will
    try,
A very large bonnet to buy;
  The neighbours will see,
  And all envy me
This very large bonnet I buy"

AUGUST 27

Little Hodge-Podge, he sat on a stile,
He thought that he would rest awhile;
He dozed, and dozed, and fell asleep,
And then fell in the ditch so deep.

AUGUST 28

Now Dolly, dear Dolly, I'll put
    you to bed;
I have a big apron, a cap on my head;
You know I'm Nurse Crabbed, and
    very severe;
So take care you are good — now mind
    that, Dolly dear.

AUGUST 29

The two twin Master Twinklebys
    Are good and quiet boys;
They neither tear their sister's hair,
    Nor do they cry for toys.

AUGUST 30

What a big umbrella! and oh, what
    a hat!
    What a curious person is he!
I've travelled for many and many
    a mile,
    Yet the like of him never did see.

AUGUST 31

Grapes, grapes! don't you like them
Purple, large and sweet!
Little children, come and pick them.
Come, and let us eat.

SEPTEMBER 1

There was an old person who heard
Some shots fired near, at a bird;
Said he, "Now I remember,
'Tis the first of September;
But there flies the fortunate bird."

SEPTEMBER 2

Here there stands a little form,
    So very lightly clad,
I really fear she will be cold;
    And it seems quite too bad.

SEPTEMBER 3

He's watching a balloon,
    That went up this afternoon;
It's gone so very high, right into
    the blue sky,
    But it's sure to come down soo

SEPTEMBER 4

This is dejected Ann,
Look at her while you can;
She will not skip, and I'm
     really fearful
She'll melt away, she is so tearful.

SEPTEMBER 5

Baby ran to meet me, she had a
     sash all blue,
A bran-new gown,
Just come from town,
A cap so crisp and new.

SEPTEMBER 6

A goodly melon,
     Colours green and yellow;
Flavour most delicious,
     Sweet and very mellow!

SEPTEMBER 7

Going to school in the morning,
     With her bag by her side, and
     her slate;
She stands and stares at the
     passers-by,
     I'm sure that she will be late.

SEPTEMBER 8

Here I am, with mallet and ball —
Who is going to play?
It is no use for me to stand
And wait for you all day.

SEPTEMBER 9

Apples, rosy-cheeked apples!
Clustering on the tree;
I'd give you one, or give you two,
If they belonged to me.

SEPTEMBER 10

Thomasina looks afar,
She sees a train go by;
"I declare that this minute I wish
I was in it,"
Thomasina said, with a sigh.

SEPTEMBER 11

Yes, see her standing there,
Watering flowers;
She loves her garden,
And works there for hours.

SEPTEMBER 12

Lawn-tennis this girl thinks a very
fine game;
Perhaps, little friends, you all think
the same;
You have to be active, and you get
very hot,
And the boys are the best at it —
now, are they not?

Speed King

SEPTEMBER 13

Just a branch with apples,
Tinted red and green;
The prettiest branch with apples
That I have ever seen.

SEPTEMBER 14

A girl sat on a wall one day,
She was tired, and would not play;
I called, "You'll fall," from the
foot of the hill,
But she paid no heed, and sat
there still.

SEPTEMBER 15

There she stands at the garden gate,
But she has come so very late;
The flowers are going, the leaves
now fall,
Twere better, perhaps, if she came
not at all.

SEPTEMBER 16

A sweet, fair maiden rested on
    the plain,
Rested, and went, and never came
    again;
Oh! little maid, now dreary is
    the spot,
Oh! little maid, 'tis there, but you
    are not.

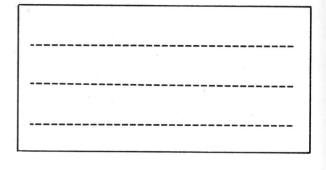

SEPTEMBER 17

Two brave stacks of famous hay,
Well stacked upon a summer day;
The birds think, as they homeward
    fly,
Some hay will keep our nests
    quite dry.

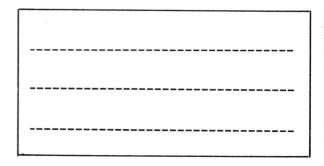

SEPTEMBER 18

Oh, dear me, what a flurry!
You seem in a desperate hurry;
    You keep up such a pace,
    Are you running in a race,
That you fly along in a scurry?

SEPTEMBER 19

Gaily dancing, tripping along,
Jumping high, and singing a song;
In your hair you've put a rose —
I think you rather want some clothes.

SEPTEMBER 20

One large apple! is it for me?
Who has picked it off the tree?
We'll have it peeled, and put in a pie,
And then we'll eat it, you and I.

SEPTEMBER 21

I should think it very hard,
    And also rather sad,
To dance alone, with so much grace
    Indeed, it is too bad.

SEPTEMBER 22

Polly has got a new Bow-wow,
    Polly is merry and gay;
Polly thinks the whole world bright,
    And this the happiest day.

SEPTEMBER 23

Digging, digging in the sands,
    With a bran-new spade;
Piling up the sand so high,
    Until a castle's made.

SEPTEMBER 24

He's trying to catch a great big fish
And then he'll put it in a dish;
He and his wife on it will sup,
Perhaps they'll eat the monster up.

SEPTEMBER 25

Reading a book with a steadfast look,
   So studiously inclined,
To run away with child and book.
   I think I've half a mind.

SEPTEMBER 26

Johnny and Julia, two good little
   things,
   Sat on the ground together;
They talked of the birds, and talked
   of the trees,
   Enjoying the sunshiny weather.

SEPTEMBER 27

A very big apple, a very large
   pear —
A nice dessert for us to share;
Let us divide them both in two,
And take two halves, both I and you.

SEPTEMBER 28

Run, run, Elizabeth, run very fast!
If you don't catch it, the ball will
    go past;
Run, run, Elizabeth! see, it will fall!
Make haste, or else you won't catch
    it at all.

SEPTEMBER 29

A large dish of grapes!
    Come, come, let us eat;
I think, for you little ones
    This is a treat.

SEPTEMBER 30

Who has been in the woods to-day?
    Who has been there a-nutting?
With long-hooked sticks, and
    baskets too;
    The branches they've been cutting.

OCTOBER 1

This is the day that the pheasants
    dread.
For the poor little things are shot
    through the head;
This little boy will help covers
    to beat,
And then there'll be plenty of
    pheasants to eat.

69

OCTOBER 2

This boy is going to sail his boat,
In a certain pond so round;
The pond is in Kensington Gardens —
You know it, I'll be bound.

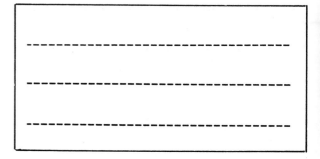

OCTOBER 3

Oh, here we are in the country!
Look at this bowl of cream!
And, you will see, five-o'clock tea
Delightful now will seem.

OCTOBER 4

Out of the sweet, sweet flowers
This funny goblin sprang;
And all the roses shook their heads,
And all the blue-bells rang.

OCTOBER 5

A girl went walking by herself,
The wind was rather high;
"Blow hard, old wind!" this bold
girl cried,
"I do not care, not I."

OCTOBER 6

Phoebe has a new battledore
    And a new shuttlecock too:
"I shall send you flying,
        shuttlecock,"
    Said Phoebe, "that's what I'll do."

OCTOBER 7

There has been rain, on the ground
        is dirt
    And so Cecilia holds up her skirt;
She holds her skirt, you see,
        quite high,
    To keep it clean, and also dry.

OCTOBER 8

A Bishop's-thumb, I do declare! —
That is the name of this queer pear;
Were I a Bishop, I should fidget,
To have so oddly-shaped a digit.

OCTOBER 9

"What are you looking at, Sally?"
        said she,
    "What do you see round there?"
"I see an old woman who rides a
        cock-horse,
    And a maiden with golden hair."

Christine

OCTOBER 10

Come and play at cricket now,
Come along, you boys;
Mind how you come, and quickly
come,
And do not make a noise.

OCTOBER 11

What fun children have,
When the horse-chesnuts come!
They peel them, and string
them —
Now go and get some.

OCTOBER 12

"Where are you going this morning?
Where are you going this morning?"
"I hear the Queen is to be seen,
And I'm going to see her this
morning."

OCTOBER 13

Here's a pear —
Not here, but there;
I mean, in the book,
If you will but look.

OCTOBER 14

What is this boy fishing for?
    What does he hope to get?
He hopes to get a very fine fish,
    But I think he will get wet.

OCTOBER 15

Why does she cry, this dear little
       trot!
    And why does she suck her thumb?
It cannot be sweet — it is horrid
       to eat;
    So, instead, let us give her a plum.

OCTOBER 16

Tabitha has a hoop to bowl,
    And Tabitha's very glad;
Tabitha had no hoop one day
    Then Tabitha was sad.

OCTOBER 17

This boy now sees a large,
      large ship,
    That's sailing out to sea;
His heart is sore, for one he loves
    Must in that large ship be.

OCTOBER 18

John and Joan go up to town,
   London town to view;
"The streets are gold, so we
     are told;
   We'll see, both I and you."

OCTOBER 19

"I've a nice new bonnet," an old
   dame said,
   "It shelters me well, I know;
Some people think it a trifle large,
   And perhaps it may be so."

OCTOBER 20

Janet didn't know her lesson,
   Janet said it badly;
Janet was rebuked severely,
   Janet took it sadly.

OCTOBER 21

"Hip, hip, hurrah!" cried Jonathan
   Green,
   "The Queen will soon pass by;
I don't care a mite for all the
    grand sight,
   But to see the Queen I'll try."

OCTOBER 22

"Ride, little brother, ride on
my back;
Where shall we go to now?
Up to the sty, to see the pig,
To the meadow to see the cow?"

OCTOBER 23

Sammy has a little line,
His mother has a dish,
On which small Sammy trusts that he
May shortly place a fish.

OCTOBER 24

Little fairy in a shell, sailing o'er
the sea!
Whither are you coming? — perhaps
to visit me.
Where, then, do you come from, o'er
the stormy main?
Little fairy, how I trust you'll get
back safe again!

OCTOBER 25

Little Polly has an old dolly,
She loves it — oh, so dearly!
She cannot see how ugly it be,
Though we can, very clearly.

OCTOBER 26

Sweet little girl, now where do
you look?
Do tell me what it can be.
"I'm looking and longing for
my Mamma,
And she is across the sea."

OCTOBER 27

Turnips, if done in this way,
Will cure a cold, so they say:
Cut the turnips into slices, put them
in a pan,
A little water, some brown sugar,
and — eat them if you can.

OCTOBER 28

Now listen, while I tell you
About this little maid,
Who went out with her Mamma —
But now it all is said.

OCTOBER 29

Little Baby's dressed, and waits —
Dressed to go a-tata;
Who do you think he's going with?
He's going out with Papa.

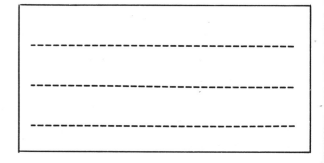

Bubby

OCTOBER 30

The leaves are turning brown and dry
They fall all round as we pass by;
The country looks all cold and drear,
No flowers, no fruit, no birds
are here.

OCTOBER 31

Stanly S.

Here's a jar of apples,
  And here we have a pan;
'Tis Allhallow E'en,
And now, I ween,
  You've all the fun you can.

NOVEMBER 1

This is little Hodge we see,
Sitting down and having tea;
Let us hope the tea is hot,
For sure it is, the weather's not.

NOVEMBER 2

Penelope goes to see her aunt,
  And sits demure and prim;
For Auntie is an ancient maid,
  Both angular and slim.

NOVEMBER 3

Here is a pair of pears!
  Cissy and you are a pair;
Let us divide the pair of pears
  Between the other pair.

NOVEMBER 4

Darling little Lily has this Birthday
    Book,
Into it the little child casts many
    and many a look;
And I know she likes it — so, I hope,
    do you;
It's made to please the children —
    that I always try to do.

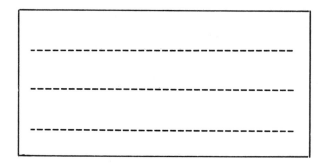

NOVEMBER 5

Remember, my friends, 'tis the
    fifth of November;
  This is a fine guy, is he not?
When such creatures we see, no
    reason there'll be,
  Why Guy Fawkes' Day should
    e'er be forgot.

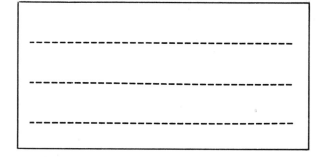

NOVEMBER 6

I stand upon the shore
And hear the great waves roar;
I see the great ships tost,
And pray that none be lost.

NOVEMBER 7

What can I give you, Ma'am, to-day?
Sausage, ham, or mutton-pie,
Beef, or tongue, chickens fine?
To please your taste, Ma'am,
I will try.

NOVEMBER 8

Leafless trees are standing bare,
Against the cold autumnal sky;
Alas, for the buds and blossoms gone
Alas, for the summer past!
we sigh.

NOVEMBER 9

What is Harry looking at,
Why does he stand and stare?
He sees a grand sight, that gives
him delight,
The Lord Mayor's Procession
is there!

NOVEMBER 10

You see, little Anna has got a
large dish
Of apples so rosy and fair;
She is coming this way, so I very
much hope
She'll invite all her friends here
to share.

NOVEMBER 11

Here's a little milkmaid,
  Very welcome, too;
Give us some nice milk to drink,
  Little milkmaid, do!

NOVEMBER 12

This girl has just come back
    from school,
  She sits and rests awhile;
She's rather tired now, you know,
  For she's walked many a mile.

NOVEMBER 13

"I must go to the stables,
  I must hie to the barn;
I must look to the horses,
  And see they come to no harm."

NOVEMBER 14

"Oh, buy my oranges! buy, I pray!
  I'm very — very poor;
You're warm and happy in your
    homes,
  I stand cold at the door."

NOVEMBER 15

A very old goblin lives in this tower,
    He eats nothing but mustard and
        batter;
And why should he choose such very
        odd fare?
    I will tell you — he's mad as a
        hatter.

NOVEMBER 16

She walked along, with her bonnet
        so big,
    And she carried her bag by
        her side,
"Ho, ho! there's a fine old girl,
        to be sure!"
    The rude street-boys then cried.

NOVEMBER 17

Polly Perkins carries a pan,
What is in it? guess, if you can;
Perhaps it's some water to wash
        her face,
But I can't say she carries the pan
        with much grace.

NOVEMBER 18

This is Miss Jessie, she looks
        rather prim,
With her nice great-coat and her
        hat so trim;
Where is she going, this cold day?
I do not know, so cannot say.

NOVEMBER 19

How cold she must be, that poor
    little mite:
    Look at her little bare arm;
I hope that Jack Frost won't give
    her a bite,
    That the weather will not do
    her harm.

NOVEMBER 20

Strike the tree, woodman,
    Strike, strike away!
Strike, strike the grand old tree,
    Strike while you may!

NOVEMBER 21

A lady went a-walking,
    She was so fair, so fair!
Alas! it is a picture,
    She is not really there.

NOVEMBER 22

Jack was such a clever boy!
    "I like to work," he said;
You see, he now goes off to school,
    To cram his busy head.

NOVEMBER 23

What do you think of her?
I think she's plain;
If you ask me once more,
I shall say so again.

NOVEMBER 24

Here's a little woman,
Carrying a large tray
Where does she come from?
Guess it now you may.

NOVEMBER 25

Little folks, here's an empty chair,
See how many of you it can bear;
Do you think two, do you think three?
I think that depends on how heavy
you be.

NOVEMBER 26

A very long dress, and a queer
frilled cap,
She carries a basket, too:
I've no more to say,
Perhaps, though, you may;
I am not so clever as you.

NOVEMBER 27

A brigand's hat! well, what of that,
  If there's no head within?
To take off one without the other,
  I really call a sin.

NOVEMBER 28

This is Obadiah,
  Who walks on the sands,
And carries a pail
  In his little hands.

NOVEMBER 29

Have pity, children, on the poor
  Their days are full of woe;
They have few clothes, so little food,
  No home where they can go.

NOVEMBER 30

There was an old man who was bent,
And over his stick he oft leant;
  He said, "But for my sticks,
  I should be in a fix,
For I really am terribly bent."

DECEMBER 1

This is a screen, a hand-screen,
    A screen that came from China!
And who do you think, now, gave
    it me?
    Why it was cousin Dinah.

DECEMBER 2

A tiny house, a nice wee house,
    A house that just suits me;
And when we're really settled there,
    I hope you'll come and see.

DECEMBER 3

Sweep, sweep, old woman,
    Sweep, sweep away;
Sweep all the dust and dirt,
    Fast as you may.

DECEMBER 4

This is Phil, who says he's ill,
    And cannot go to school;
He's running just the other way:
    He will grow up a fool.

DECEMBER 5

On a cold, cold day in December,
    Delightful it is, to be sure,
To sit in front of the fire;
    But take care there's no draught
        from the door.

DECEMBER 6

This is Angelina, going for a walk,
She can smile so pleasantly, and so
    nicely talk;
She is indeed so sweet a child, that
    like her there are few,
She is a dear good little girl, and
    so, perhaps, are you.

DECEMBER 7

Here's a handsome cup, I wonder
    what is in it?
Give a guess now, children, say
    what you think, this minute;
Lily says it's chocolate, Johnny says
    it's tea;
Now, children, what do you say?
    Please to tell it me.

DECEMBER 8

Certainly she's tall and slight,
Certainly a weight quite light;
Certainly I don't admire
This tall, straight dame, or her
    attire.

DECEMBER 9

Poor little beggar-girl, out in the
cold!
Show pity, all you who have silver
and gold;
Give from your plenty all you can
spare,
With the poor and the wretched be
willing to share.

DECEMBER 10

A broom in his hand, a mop on
his head,
A little merry boy;
Few playthings he has, so he takes
the broom,
To serve him for a toy.

DECEMBER 11

This is good Mr. Longnose,
For his learning famed, and
sense;
P'rhaps the knowledge he has gained
Has made his nose immense.

DECEMBER 12

See, what a poor little ragged lad!
It really makes me very sad
To see a boy in such a state;
Now think, how very hard his fate.

DECEMBER 13

Phoebe sits upon a stool,
  Of legs it has but three;
It may be big enough for her,
  But not for you or me.

DECEMBER 14

Here we are on a cold, cold night,
Rolled up warm, so nice and tight:
Going off to see a play,
At the close of a winter's day.

DECEMBER 15

What do you want now, Billy?
What do you want, I say?
  "I've been a good boy,
  So I want a toy,
And a plum-bun this day."

DECEMBER 16

Here's a merry lad, I ween,
Happy he, as King or Queen;
Glad is he to take your penny,
Still he smiles if you've not any.

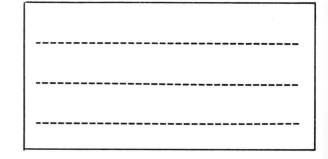

DECEMBER 17

A coachman ready for the road,
    Wrapped up from chin to toes;
He has something tragic on his mind,
    Which troubles ere he goes.

DECEMBER 18

I think we come upon a fancy ball,
Or else I cannot make him out at all;
His curious hat, with large and
    drooping feather,
His dress, unsuited to the time or
    weather.

DECEMBER 19

A Dresden china figure this,
    How pretty, children—look!
We really find some curious things
    Within this Birthday Book.

DECEMBER 20

And where do you come from, with
    shillalagh in your hand?
"Shure, and plase yer honor, I come
    from Paddyland,
Auld Ireland, the island of praties
    and milk;
And shure, blarney, too—ain't our
    tongues soft as silk?"

DECEMBER 21

What archer is this? Why, bold
    Robin Hood;
He has left all his men, and come
    out of the wood;
He thought you would like to handle
    the bow,
So the best way to do so he thought
    he would show.

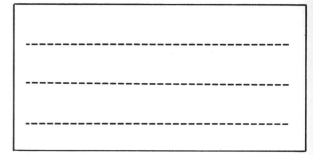

DECEMBER 22

This is Hang-me-up-hi, the
    mandarin,
As grand a Chinese as ever
    was seen;
Look at his pigtail, look at his toes,
And all his very magnificent clothes.

DECEMBER 23

Here's another little fellow,
    In fancy dress you see;
A little cavalier, I think
    That he must really be.

DECEMBER 24

Christmas Eve! Now, all you merry
    children,
    Hang up your stockings, and sink
      to happy rest,
Then gliding through the room the
    Christ-child passes,
    And breathing near the sleepers,
      leaves them blest.

DECEMBER 25

Christmas! Hear the joy-bells
    ringing,
Glad hymns in the churches singing;
Of His mercy, of His power,
And the gifts good angels shower!

DECEMBER 26

Why does she wear a steeple stuck
    upon her head?
This is a mediaeval dress, so
    I've heard it said;
Why has she got a battledore and
    shuttlecock in hand?
To tell the truth, this lady I cannot
    understand.

DECEMBER 27

A person once said "I will run;
You can have no idea of the fun
    Of running so fast
    That you drop down at last,
And feel that you're utterly done."

DECEMBER 28

Little Bo-peep, I declare,
    With little hat and crook!
How nice to find so old a friend
    Within the Birthday Book.

DECEMBER 29

Yes, I was sure of it, sure as
　　could be,
And yet he would not listen to me;
He kicked his legs, and he made
　　them sore,
With those ridiculous spurs he wore.

DECEMBER 30

This looks to me like a dreadful
　　robber;
　　Is it he who left the "Babes in
　　　the Wood"
To perish sadly with cold and hunger,
　　Covered with leaves by the dickies
　　　good?

DECEMBER 31

This old woman takes a fly,
To sweep the cobwebs off the sky.
She says, "As I'm going up so high,
I wish the Old Year, and you all,
　　Good-bye."